The Creek at the Farm

Story by Annette Smith
Illustrations by Samantha Asri

Josh and Lily were staying at Grandpa's farm for the holidays.

"Let's go down to the creek, Josh, and look for tadpoles," said Lily.

"No, Lily," said Josh.
"Grandpa told us not to go down there without him."

Lucky, Grandpa's dog,
came running over to them.
He jumped up at Josh and started to bark.

"Why are you barking, Lucky?"
said Josh, giving him a pat.

Lily patted Lucky too, but he still kept barking.

Lucky ran over to the farm gate.

"Come on, Josh!" shouted Lily.
"Let's see where he goes."

Lucky ran very fast down the hill
to the creek.

"Grandpa is going to be cross with us,"
said Josh.

Then, the children saw a little calf
down by the creek.
It was stuck in the mud.

“Where is its mother?” said Lily.

“She’s over there, behind the fence!”
said Josh.

“We have to help the little calf,” said Lily.

“No, Lily,” said Josh. “We **can’t** go down there.
Let’s run back and get Grandpa.”

Josh and Lily ran back to the farm house.

"Grandpa! Grandpa!" shouted Josh. "A little calf is stuck in the mud by the creek."

"You need to help it," said Lily. "The little calf can't get back to its mother!"

"I'll get the farm bike," said Grandpa.
"If you want to see me pull out the calf,
then stay under the big tree
up on the hill.
Don't come down to the creek."

Josh and Lily waited under the tree
with Lucky.

Grandpa was very careful
as he lifted the little calf out of the mud.

Then he walked over to the fence
and put it down by its mother.

"The little calf will be happy now,"
said Lily.

"Yes, it will," said Josh.

“The little calf won’t get out again,”
said Grandpa,
when he came back up the hill.
“I have fixed the hole in the fence.”

"Lucky, you are a clever dog," said Josh.

"Yes, he is," said Lily.
"But we won't go down to the creek again without you, Grandpa."

"That's good," said Grandpa with a smile.

Narrator

Matt, Cam and Sarah always have fun playing music together. They have decided to try busking at the local arts festival. Sarah has been online looking for tips on busking. On the day, they set off nice and early to secure their spot.

Matt

Our spot is just down here, right next to the wall …
Oh, no! Someone's beaten us to it!

Cam

Oh! What? No!

Matt's mum

Quick, there's another spot just down the road – right opposite The Early Inn Café.

Dad and I can sit there while we watch you.

Sarah

That's not nearly as good as this one! This is where the most people are.

When I researched busking online, I found out that choosing a good position is really important.

Cam

Well, what are you going to do, push him out of the way?

Quick! Run!

Narrator

They all rushed down the road and set up before anyone else came along.

Matt put down his open guitar case to collect the money. They hoped that by the end of the session it would be full.

Matt's dad

Here, I'll put in some coins. That should encourage people to throw money in it.

Matt *(sounding hopeful)*

If you put in a five-dollar note, they might be encouraged to donate more.

Matt's dad

Good try, Matt. Your mother and I will be sitting right across the road at the café. Good luck!

Matt

Couldn't you sit at a different café? Maybe one a bit further away?

We don't want you staring at us and grinning, the way parents do.

Matt's mum *(hiding a smile)*

We won't look at you. We'll just listen.

Narrator

Matt, Cam and Sarah actually felt a bit nervous – but they tried not to show it.

Matt played a few chords and re-tuned a couple of strings.

Cam played a few scales on the keyboard as they discussed their approach.

Sarah *(taking a deep breath)*

Now, remember, this kind of busking is called a continuous performance. We have to try to engage the audience, but they probably won't stay for more than a couple of songs. It's not like an act with a starting and ending point.

Cam

We know, Sarah. You've only told us that about ten times. We're not starting a business you know.

Matt

Let's just get going. If we don't start playing, everyone will find someone else to watch.

(to Sarah)

Sarah, are you ready? You need to stop raving and get ready to introduce the first song. Try to get people to stop and watch.

Sarah *(muttering to herself)*

Let me have a practice.

Um … hi, everyone! We're the Seascape Trio, and we're … *Aaarrgh!*

I mean, we're the Sea**side** Trio, and we're here today to … to …

Cam *(encouragingly)*

… to entertain you with a few of our favourite songs.

Sarah

To entertain you with a few of our favourites. We're going to start off with … with …

What are we starting with, again?

Matt

With a number by Two Dimension. *Sarah!* For someone who spent hours online finding out about busking, you're not very well prepared. Have you got stage fright?

Cam

Hold it, everyone. We can't start yet. The mic isn't working.

Sarah

What! The *mic* isn't working?

That was Point Number Two on the busking list! "Check that all equipment is in good working order!" It was right after Point Number One: "Select a repertoire of songs that showcases your style and that is likely to attract an audience."

Cam *(exasperated)*

We know!

Matt

Don't panic. It's fixed. The switch wasn't in the "on" position. Okay, Sarah – do the intro and we'll go straight into the first song.

Sarah *(very loudly)*

Hi, everyone! We're the Seaside Trio, and today we're going to entertain you with a few of our favourites. Let's begin with a number by Two Dimension!

Cam *(out of the side of his mouth)*

That was great, Sarah, but you don't have to yell. You nearly took my ear off. The mic is working now, remember?

Narrator

After the first couple of numbers, the members of the Seaside Trio were feeling a bit more confident. But … they had earned only two dollars, and nobody had stayed to listen for long.

Sarah came up with another idea.

Sarah

We need to seize people's attention. According to what I read on the internet, movement and colour is important. How about I do a few dance moves with the tambourine?

Matt

Well … as long as you don't look like an idiot.

Sarah

Of course not.

Just like this …

and this …

and this …

Cam *(laughing)*

Ahem. You do realise you have an audience but, unfortunately, not the kind that throws money.

Sarah

Oh no! It's Emily and Alyssa! I can't sing and dance with my friends watching. They're waving at me. How embarrassing!

Matt

Weren't you the one telling us how important it is to behave in a professional manner?

Ignore them. I'm going to start playing now.

Ready? You'd better be in time with that tambourine.

Sarah

I can't do this …

Narrator

Sarah managed to overcome her embarrassment and put in a good performance.

Unfortunately, the only three people who stood still to listen were her friends Emily and Alyssa … and a man with a bike.

Then, something else happened.

A performing troupe set up near Matt, Cam and Sarah.

Really, it seemed that it was not The Seaside Trio's day.

Matt

Uh, oh!

It seems we have competition!

Cam

It's a performing troupe! We might as well pack up and go home.

Matt

Look, they've got acrobats and stilt walkers. And firesticks! Wow, look at that girl juggle!

Sarah

Are we going to stand here watching another act or are we going to perform like professionals?

Cam *(distracted)*

Did you see how high he jumped? Oh, I see, that was just to get everyone's attention.

Now they're getting someone from the crowd to join in.

Sarah

Look, everyone is leaving us to watch *them*.

Matt

"Everyone"?

Do you mean that one man with the bike?

Sarah

See, what they're doing is called a circle act. Their act has a starting and finishing point – like magic tricks. Ours is just a walk-by.

Cam *(laughing)*

That's what our audience is doing all right.

Walking right on by.

Sarah

We need to *sing*.
We're not giving up.

Narrator

Our trio kept singing.

After an hour, they had made exactly four dollars and seventy cents.

They were feeling a bit downhearted.

As they packed up, they discussed whether they should try again.

Then they heard a voice call out.

It was a waitress from the café across the road.

Waitress *(waving)*

Hey! Kids!

Cam, Sarah and Matt *(all together)*

Hi.

Waitress

You were all really good! Our customers loved it. Are you coming back tomorrow?

Matt *(looking at the others)*

Um … are we?

Cam *(grins)*

Why not?

OPEN

Sarah *(calls to waitress)*

Sure we are! See you!

(to the others)

What did I tell you?

This is just the start of a brilliant career!

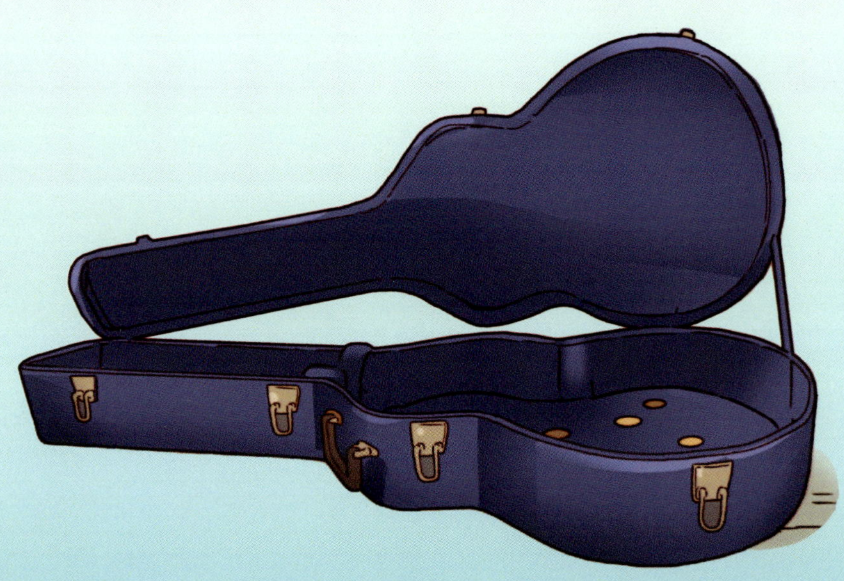

● REC

Movie Mania

By Marg McAlister

Illustrated by Lyn Stone

Characters:

Narrator

Dad

Jack

Mum

Henry
Jack's brother

Grace
Jack's sister

Narrator

After watching the latest box-office hit movie, Jack Summers has a revelation about what he wants to do with his life. He is going to be a movie director! He talks about it so much that his parents give him a video camera for his birthday. But now, some of the family are beginning to wonder whether that was such a good idea.

You see, Jack, has just announced his first movie is going to be about his family – *A Day in the Life of the Summers' Family.* Jack explains his movie concept to his family as they all sit in the kitchen.

Jack

Okay, everyone. The idea is to make the movie seem really natural and lifelike.

You just do whatever you usually would do. You'll hardly notice me.

Grace

I hope this doesn't mean you'll be spying on us?

Mum

Oh, come on, Grace. Play along with it.

Just think: one day we'll be all going along to the Oscars to see Jack win "Best Director".

Henry

What do we have to do? We don't have to talk to the camera, do we?

Jack *(sighing)*

I don't want you to perform for the camera. Just be natural. Pretend you can't see me.

Grace

This is going to be the most boring movie in the history of the world.

Narrator

Finally everyone gets sick of staring at Jack and his video camera and they all disperse.

Jack walks outside to take a location shot of the house. Then he walks inside to see what his family is doing.

Jack

(to himself as he mimes filming)

The family is all at home today, so let's go and see what they're up to.

I'm walking through the front door of the Summers' house.

I'm walking down the hall … and into the kitchen.

● REC

Jack

Hmm, nobody's in the kitchen. Where did they all go?

I'll see if I can find my brother Henry. He's nine, a year younger than I am.

Hmm, he's not in his room … I'll keep walking …

Henry!

What are you doing in my room and on my computer?

Henry

Nothing! I mean, just looking at your new video editing program to see how it works.

Jack

Don't touch it! I've got it set up how I like it.

Henry

I'm not hurting it.

You never let me use your things.

Here, film this: Jack is the meanest brother ever.

Jack

Oh, very mature, Henry. Get your face out of my camera.

REC

Narrator

Well, videoing the first family member didn't go so well.

Jack keeps filming, and finds his mother in the family room.

She's trying out some New Age exercise routines that are a mix between yoga and tai chi.

She pretends that she doesn't notice Jack, but he sees her sneak a glance at the camera.

Mum

And one – and two – and slowly down …

And three – and four – and slowly, slowly up …

And five – and six – flow gently on to the right foot …

And seven – and eight – the right hand floats slowly out to point to the sun …

Jack *(whispering)*

Ah, this is good. Just the sort of footage I wanted.

Narrator

Suddenly, the family cat shoots through the door, causing Jack's mother to trip and fall onto her yoga mat.

Mum

Aaarrgh!

Ouch! Jack, you let the cat in!

Jack *(trying not to laugh)*

Oops! Sorry, I didn't realise. Are you all right?

Mum *(sarcastically)*

Well, thanks very much for helping me up.

Ouch. Ouch.

Ignore that footage, Jack. I'll start over again.
Are you ready?

Jack

The video is still running. Are you okay?

Mum

Yes, I'm fine, but you can't film me falling over.

Wait, let me do it again.

I was getting really good at this …

Jack

Mum, please … I'm the director here. That means that I am the driving creative force. I interpret what I see so it expresses my vision. I don't want perfection. I want it to be real.

Mum *(firmly)*

We'll talk about this later! Now, film it again with me doing it properly.

Narrator

Jack knows that tone of his mother's voice.

He obediently films his mother doing her moves flawlessly and then closes the door.

Narrator

Jack can hear his sister's voice in her bedroom. She's using that artificial giggly voice that she uses on the phone. It's the voice she uses to talk to her friends about boys.

Jack *(to himself)*

Hmm, I think this could be good …

Grace *(miming being on a mobile)*

Oh, I know, tell me about it! Did you notice how long his eyelashes are? It's not fair; I would kill for eyelashes like that.

And that dimple. Don't you love his dimple? *(pause)*

I *know*. *(giggles)* Really? Really? He told you he likes me? Ryan Corby? What did he say? Did he –

Grace *(to Jack)*

Hey! Stop that!

(miming speaking into her mobile)

Wait a minute, Emma, it's my annoying brother. Let me just get rid of him.

Narrator

Grace puts the mobile to one side to speak to her brother.

Grace *(hissing at Jack)*

I *told* you not to spy on me!

Jack

I'm not spying! I'm making a film. I told you – Grace, let the camera go!

Grace

You – are – not – using – that footage!

Jack

Sorry, Sis, you can't dictate what I can and can't use.

As a director, I will be ultimately responsible for this film's artistic success or failure … let go of my camera!

Grace, stop it. I've stopped filming, okay?

Narrator

Jack's first artistic endeavour isn't going so well.

Well, there's still his father.

Jack can hear him in the kitchen, muttering to himself. That usually means he is trying to fix something.

Jack

(miming speaking to camera)

What this family doesn't understand is that a film director like myself has a higher level of artistic vision than most people. It's very difficult trying to communicate that to my family.

They all want to look perfect, but that doesn't fit with my aim of creating an engaging film. *(sighs)*

Let's see what my father is up to …
Ah, under the kitchen sink with a wrench.
This should be good.

Dad *(grunting and talking to himself)*

C'mon, give way, can't you … C'mon, c'mon … just a little bit more …

Got you!

Now where'd I put that new pipe? Ah, there it is!

C'mon, I know you fit. I measured it.

That's it, slot in there.

Oh, I'm good.

Jack *(whispering)*

This is the stage where something usually goes wrong.

Okay, he's about to turn on the water.

It's lake-on-the-kitchen-floor time …

Dad *(to Jack)*

It worked!

Jack! Did you see that? Better still, did you get it on film?

The first time ever I've fixed a kitchen drainage problem!

Hello, viewers. I am Pete Summers and I am the best amateur plumber in the suburb. In the city. In the state!

Jack

Well, at least one member of this family is cooperative.

Narrator

Jack turns around to find his mother, sister and brother surrounding him.

Mum

You are not putting that footage of me falling over into a movie.

I know you. It'll end up on the internet.

Grace

And that's the same for me, Jack.

You may find that your nice new video camera is held hostage.

Henry

And I've already told you, I don't want to be in your silly old film.

Narrator

Jack has a difficult time trying to edit, with all the family hovering over his shoulder, demanding he cut their scenes.

To keep the peace, Jack finally agrees to cut back his film.

He plays his finished film to his family. Unfortunately, after all the cuts, the film is only about two minutes long.

His father is, of course, the star – he likes his scene.

When the film ends, his satisfied family leaves, and Jack turns the camera on himself.

Jack

Hello, viewers. You have just seen my first final cut – as approved by the actors.

Unfortunately, my family just didn't understand my creative vision.

But I'm sure you know what happens to some of the footage that is edited out.

Yes, that's right … you see them when the credits roll.

Keep watching. It's time for the bloopers!

REC

REC

REC

REC